Dinosaur Hide, Dinosaur Seek

Written by Lisa Regan

Brown Watson
ENGLAND

First published 2016 by Brown Watson
The Old Mill, 76 Fleckney Road
Kibworth Beauchamp
Leicestershire LE8 0HG
ISBN: 978-0-7097-2320-2
© 2016 Brown Watson, England
Reprinted 2017
Printed in Malaysia

Dinky the dinosaur is looking for her friends.
They are playing hide and seek.

Dinky loves to play. She closes
her eyes and counts to ten.

1 – 2 – 3 – 4 – 5 – 6 – 7 – 8 – 9 – 10.
'Coming, ready or not!' she roars.

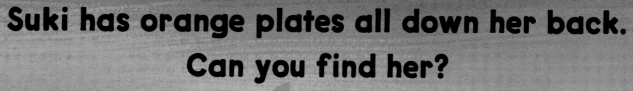

**Suki has orange plates all down her back.
Can you find her?**

'I can see you!' laughs Dinky.
Suki laughs too. She jumps out from behind a rock.

Together, they look for their friends.
Where can they be hiding?

They walk over to the waterfall.
They are looking for Archie.

Archie has a pointed tail with spikes on it. Can you find him?

'I can see you!' laughs Dinky.
Archie laughs too. He likes
it underneath the water!

Together, they look for their friends.
Where can they be hiding?

They wander into the woods.
They are looking for Roxy.

Roxy has a spotted crest on top of her head. Can you find her?

'I can see you!' laughs Dinky.
Roxy laughs too. She waves
from behind the tree.

Together, they look for their friends.
Where can they be hiding?

They march towards the mountains.
They are looking for Tricky.

Tricky has a horn on the end of his nose. Can you find him?

'I can see you!' laughs Dinky. Tricky laughs too. He likes it inside the cave!

Together, they look for their friends.
Where can they be hiding?

They ramble down to the river.
They are looking for Pebbles.

Pebbles has a purple bony
patch on top of her head.
Dinky can't see her.

The friends look high and low.
'Pebbles, where are you?' they shout.

They search and search but Pebbles
is nowhere to be found.

When they get back, they find Pebbles.
She has gone home for lunch!